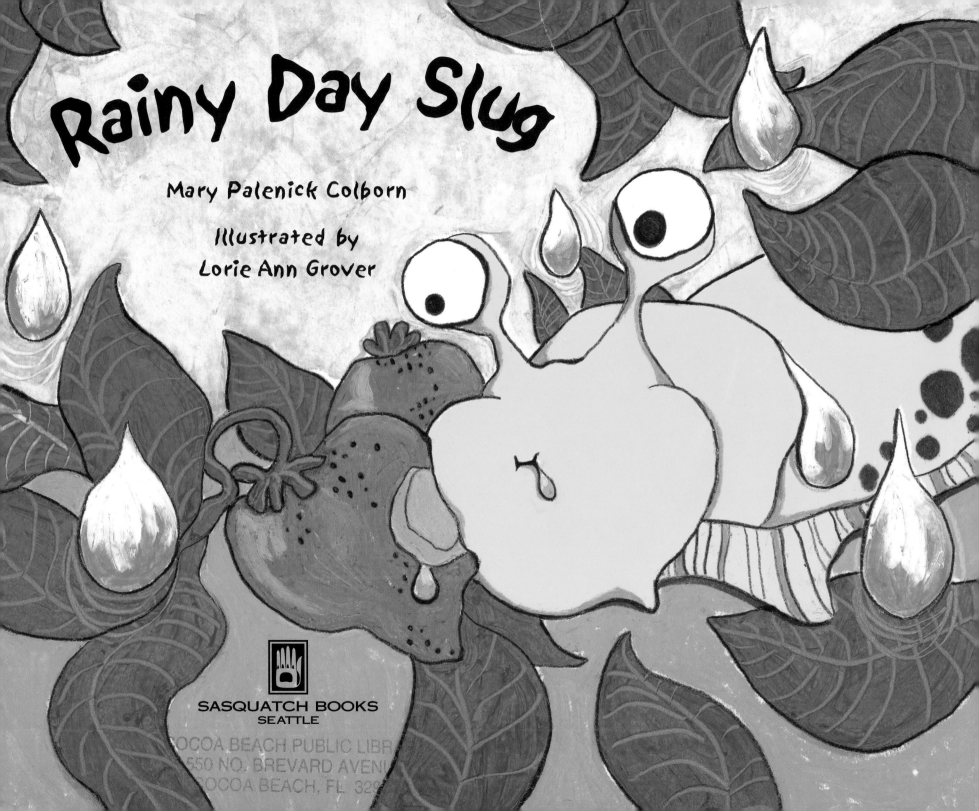

Rainy Day Slug

Mary Palenick Colborn

Illustrated by
Lorie Ann Grover

SASQUATCH BOOKS
SEATTLE

It went scrass, scrass, scrass

through the tall, green grass

in a deep rain puddle

into a tiny, hidden crack

over the soft, blue rug

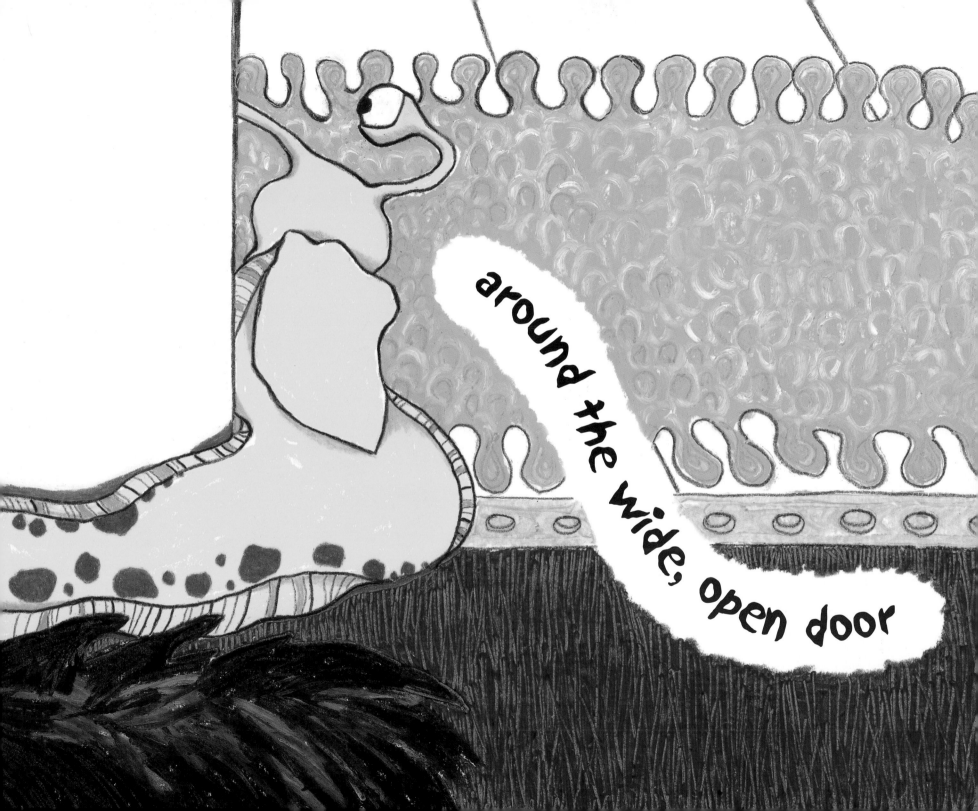

across the cold, white tile

by old Father Time

for a slug on a walk

Hi! I'm a banana slug and live in the Northwest. The scenes in this book of my garden home and strawberry diet are actually not true. Because I'm native to the region, I don't eat your garden fruit or vegetables. That's the work of nasty invaders, like the European black slug. I prefer woodland habitats and am the second-largest slug in the world, sometimes growing to as long as ten inches!

For Mattie, the first and foremost slug lover. –M.P.C.

For my girls, Emily and Ellen. –L.A.G.

Text copyright ©2000 by Mary Palenick Colborn
Illustrations copyright ©2000 by Lorie Ann Grover

Printed in Hong Kong
Distributed in Canada by Raincoast Books, Ltd.
04 03 02 01 00   5 4 3 2 1

Library of Congress Cataloging in Publication Data
Colborn, Mary Palenick
Rainy day slug/by Mary Palenick Colborn; illustrations by Lorie Ann Grover.
p. cm.
Summary: One rainy day, a slug goes for a walk in the wide, wide world, going scrass, scrass, scrass through the tall, green grass, scuddle, scuddle, scuddle in a deep rain puddle, and scrape, scrape, scrape down a long, pink drape.
ISBN 1-57061-238-2 (alk. paper)
[1. Slugs (Mollusks)—Fiction. 2. Stories in rhyme.]
I. Grover, Lorie Ann, ill. II. Title.

PZ8.3.C6655 Rai 2000
[E]—dc21
99-047253

Sasquatch Books
615 Second Avenue
Seattle, Washington 98104
(206) 467-4300
www.SasquatchBooks.com